This book belongs to

....

As the film progresses, Moana regains a connection to her wayfinder ancestors. **ANDY HARKNESS / DIGITAL**

NEYSA BOVÉ / DIGITAL (previous and 70–71)

◎ **MODERN CLASSICS** ◎

Disney

MOANA

Acknowledgments

Special thanks to Walt Disney Animation Studios and Walt Disney Animation Research Library
for their invaluable assistance and for providing the artwork for this book.

First published in the UK in 2023 by Studio Press Books,
an imprint of Bonnier Books UK,
4th Floor, Victoria House, Bloomsbury Square,
London WC1B 4DA
Owned by Bonnier Books,
Sveavägen 56, Stockholm, Sweden
bonnierbooks.co.uk

Copyright © 2023 Disney Enterprises, Inc.
All rights reserved. No part of this publication may be
reproduced or transmitted in any form or by any means,
electronic, or mechanical, including photocopying, recording,
or by any information storage and retrieval system,
without permission in writing from the publisher.

Printed in China
2 4 6 8 10 9 7 5 3 1

All rights reserved
ISBN 978-1-80078-563-2

Text adapted by Sally Morgan
Edited by Ellie Rose and Frankie Jones
Designed by Rob Ward and Maddox Philpot
Cover illustrated by Chellie Carroll
Production by Emma Kidd

A CIP catalogue record is available from the British Library

My admiration for animation started as a child growing up in Michigan, watching all the Disney animated films. Although these films left a big impression on me, I never thought I would be part of making these films myself. It really hadn't occurred to me that these beautiful characters were images created by humans.

After all, they were living, breathing characters who had feelings, thoughts and a point of view. It wasn't until my 3rd year of art school that I took an animation course, and I instantly fell in love with the art of animation.

My path into animation did not come easily or quickly, and despite my recent successes, I've learned that animation is a life-long journey. You never really know it all, you just keep learning. As a new Head of Animation on the film *Moana*, I was unsure of my abilities. I lacked the confidence in my potential as I was surrounded by so many talented artists that I felt could do a better job than me. I think this is why I love and admire Moana's character so much. She is tenacious and brave. She believes in herself and never gives up on her journey to save her people. She goes way beyond the boundaries, and learns that her strength comes from within herself.

While I have not always believed in myself, I learned through my opportunity on *Moana* to listen to my voice and find my own strength. I've learned the importance of knowing who you are and what you bring to the table. For me, this internal journey started on *Moana* and it is a lesson that has stayed with me to this very day and will continue into the future.

Moana taught us that only you can choose how far you'll go. As you read through the story, you'll see her journey of conquering many challenges. These require her to find strength, believe in herself and know that she is capable of anything she puts her mind to. I hope you will find inspiration, learn from her courageousness and most of all believe in yourself. You will be the one to decide who you really are!

Amy Lawson Smeed
Head of Animation
Walt Disney Animation Studios

MODERN CLASSICS

On the tropical island of Motunui, a silver haired woman named Gramma Tala stood in a thatched structure called a *fale* and told the story of her people.

'In the beginning, there was only ocean,' Gramma Tala said as village children listened. Gramma Tala used the *tapa* cloths that decorated the fale to illustrate her story. As Gramma Tala spoke, her words brought the images on the cloths to life.

One day, out of this endless ocean, an island emerged. The island was a beautiful goddess named Te Fiti. Te Fiti's heart had the power to create life. Te Fiti shared this power with the world.

Gramma Tala is one of the oldest people on Motunui. She is the most connected to the islander's past and their history of navigation. JIN KIM / DIGITAL

When developing Te Fiti, Andy Harkness, art director of environments, worked with clay to sculpt an outline that reflected the body of the goddess Te Fiti.
ANDY HARKNESS / CLAY SCULPT (TOP), ANDY HARKNESS / DIGITAL (BOTTOM)

As Te Fiti grew, the shape of her body formed verdant mountains and valleys. At the centre of this paradise, Te Fiti's heart shone, filling the world with life.

Gramma Tala said that time passed and some became jealous of Te Fiti's heart. These wicked creatures wanted to steal the heart and its life-giving power.

One day, the most daring of those wishing to take the heart sailed across the ocean and did just that. This trickster was Maui – a demigod with the power to transform himself with his magical fishhook.

Modern Classics

Maui transformed into a hawk to fly to Te Fiti, where he became a lizard to crawl through her grass. Maui became a bug to squeeze through rocks. On the other side, Maui revealed himself as a powerful demigod with flowing black hair. Maui prised the heart from Te Fiti and smiled as he flipped it into the air, but when he caught it, the earth began to shake.

'Without her heart, the island of Te Fiti crumbled, giving birth to a terrible darkness,' Gramma Tala said.

The once green and beautiful island turned to dust. Maui ran, but his path was blocked by another who wanted the heart. This creature was Te Kā – a demon of earth and fire.

Gramma Tala is a natural storyteller. Her quirky character contrasts with that of her son, Chief Tui.
Bill Schwab / Digital

Maui leapt to fight Te Kā but was blasted from the sky and never seen again. Also lost were Maui's fishhook and Te Fiti's heart, which sank deep beneath the ocean's waves.

Gramma Tala told the children that Te Kā was still out there. The darkness that began when Te Fiti's heart was stolen was getting closer, draining the life from everything until it consumed them all.

Terrified, the children stared at the old woman, except one little girl – Gramma Tala's granddaughter, Moana, clapped her hands and smiled for more.

One day, Gramma Tala said, a person brave enough to sail beyond the reef surrounding their island would find Maui, restore the heart to Te Fiti and save them all.

Hearing this, Chief Tui strode into the fale and told his mother that they'd had enough stories. He assured the children that no one from Motunui ever sailed outside of the reef and said there were no monsters or darkness.

But as he said this, Chief Tui bumped into the side of the fale, causing the tapa cloths to unfurl and reveal pictures of terrifying creatures, plunging them all into darkness. The children screamed.

Chief Tui told the children that they were safe on the island. But Gramma Tala said that the legends were true. As Chief Tui and Gramma Tala argued, Moana crawled away to the beach.

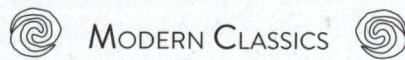

Modern Classics

Moana toddled towards the waves and saw a shell. Moana bent to collect it, but heard screeching behind her. Hungry birds were waiting for a baby turtle to emerge from the bushes. Moana wanted the shell, but the turtle needed help. Moana used a leaf to shield the turtle and guide it to safety.

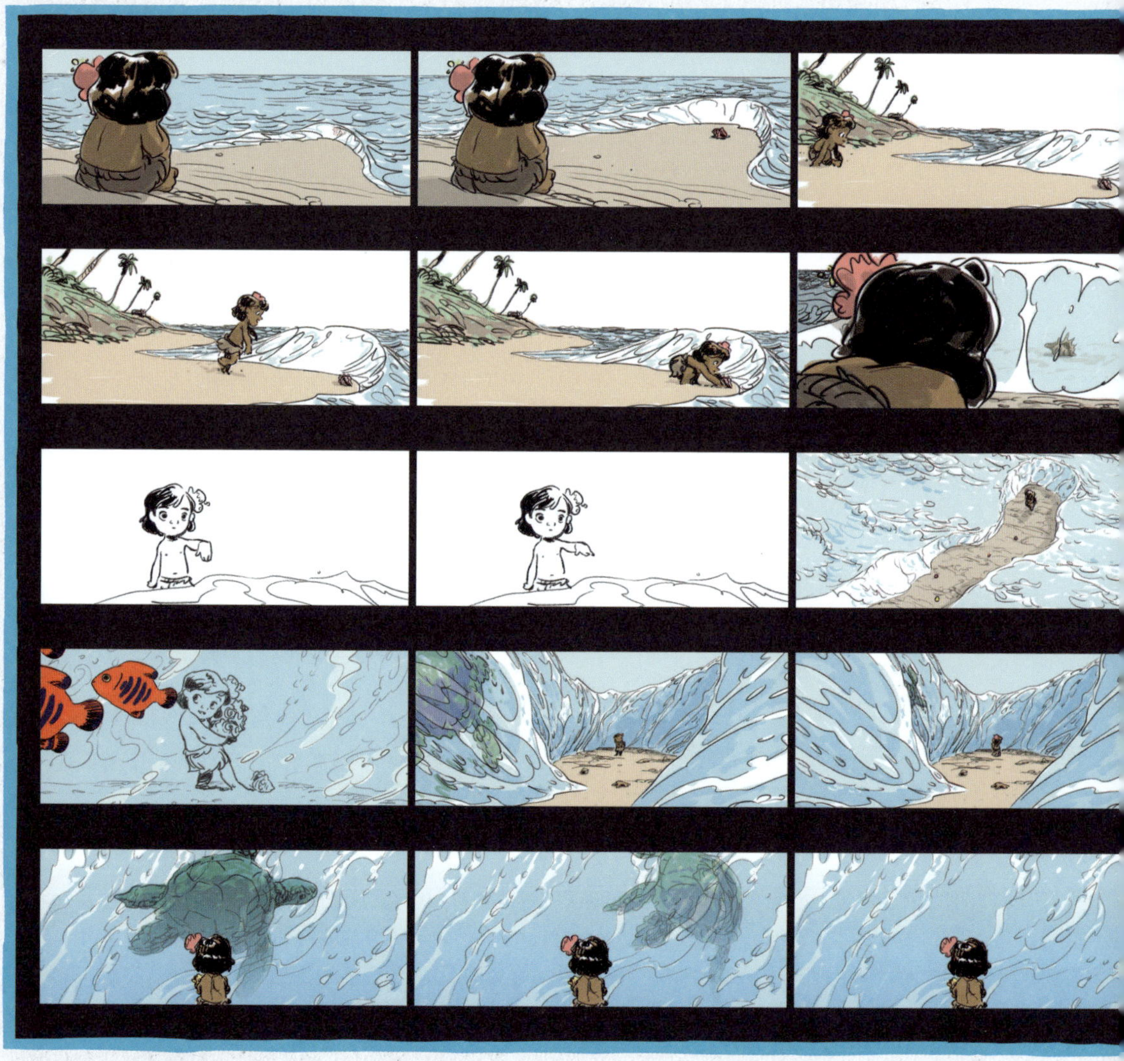

This storyboard by co-director Chris Williams shows the first time a young Moana meets her best friend, the ocean. **Chris Williams / Digital**

As the turtle swam away, the ocean rippled with magic and the waves parted to reveal the shell. Moana picked it up and spied another. As Moana walked towards it, the ocean opened itself to her. When her arms were full of shells, a wave rose up in front of her. Moana looked at it and the wave looked back. Moana touched the wave and giggled as the water trickled on to her. The wave engulfed Moana's hair, topping it with a pink flower, but that wasn't all. The ocean had something else for Moana.

Moana looked into the ocean and saw a green jewel in the water. Moana reached out and took it – it was the heart of Te Fiti from Gramma Tala's story. At that moment, Moana heard her father.

The ocean floated Moana to shore. When Moana landed she stumbled, and dropped the heart. Moana reached for it, but before she could get it, her father scooped her up.

'You scared me,' her father said.

Moana wanted to go back, but her father said the ocean was dangerous.

As they walked to the village, Chief Tui told Moana that one day she would be chief. Moana's mother, Sina, told her she would do wonderful things as chief. But first, Moana needed to learn about the island.

Modern Classics

Moana's father believed that that there was no need to explore the ocean, because they had everything they needed right there. The people of Motunui were resourceful and worked together to make what they needed from what they could find on the island. Everything on the island had a use and nothing went to waste. Coconuts were used for food, their fibres were used to make nets, and their leaves were used to make fires.

As Moana grew up, Chief Tui taught her all about the island's many traditions. He hoped that when she became chief she would maintain them, just as he did.

Moana loved the island, but her heart always brought her back to the ocean.

Motunui is a tropical island surrounded by a barrier reef. Moana's ancestors have called the island home for thousands of years. **Kevin Nelson / Digital**

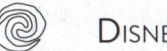 DISNEY MOANA

Whenever Moana could escape from her duties, she ran to the shore to be with her Gramma Tala who liked to dance by the ocean. Many in the village thought this was strange, but Gramma Tala was doing what made her happy. Gramma Tala wanted the same for Moana. She told Moana to follow the voice inside her, no matter what. One day, Gramma Tala told Moana that this voice was who she really was and that Moana should follow it, even if it told her to travel across the ocean and disobey her father. Gramma Tala took Moana to the boats on the shore, but as Moana walked towards them, her father stopped her.

Chief Tui led Moana to a sacred place at the top of a mountain. There, Moana saw a mysterious tower of flat stones, placed on top of one another.

Modern Classics

Since settling on Motunui, the villagers no longer travel past the reef encircling the island. In order to have enough food to eat, they began farming the land. **Nick Orsi / Digital**

Chief Tui told her that each stone was put there by a chief of Motunui. Chief Tui had put a stone there, as had his father and his grandfather. He said that one day it would be Moana's turn.

'You are the future of our people, Moana. And they are not out there,' he said pointing to the ocean. 'They are right here. It is time to be who they need you to be.'

As months passed, Moana put all of her efforts into learning to be a good leader. Moana's parents were proud of her – she still longed for the ocean

The villagers' outfits reflect the fact they have lived on the island for many years. The plants they use are dried and they have time to create beautiful, intricate pieces. **Bobby Pontillas / Digital**

but tried to stay focused. Moana did what she could to help people with their problems, fixing fales, teaching children and caring for animals.

Among these animals were a piglet name Pua and a rooster named Heihei. One of the villagers thought Heihei was stupid and wanted to cook him, but Moana would not let him.

Many of the islanders outfits are made from *tapa*, a type of bark cloth that is used throughout Oceania to make clothing and domestic items. **Nick Orsi / Digital**

Life was good in Motunui, but things were changing. One day, a woman came to Moana with a coconut filled with ash. The woman told Moana that all the coconuts were filled with ash so Moana decided they would clear the affected trees and plant a new grove.

'This suits you.' Chief Tui said, proud of his daughter's leadership.

But coconuts weren't the only problem facing Motunui. A fisherman told Moana and her father that the traps in the lagoon were catching fewer fish. Moana suggested they try fishing elsewhere in the lagoon, but the fisherman said it was no use. 'They're just gone,' the fisherman said.

Modern Classics

Moana looked to the ocean as her father told the fisherman that he would take the matter to the council and see what they could do.

'What if we fished beyond the reef?' Moana asked.

'No one goes beyond the reef,' her father said sternly.

Moana didn't understand. If there were no fish in the lagoon, then surely they needed to travel beyond the reef to look for them. But her father insisted it was a rule that kept them safe. He was angry with Moana for suggesting something that could put people's lives in danger, and disappointed that once again her thoughts were on the ocean.

'No one goes beyond the reef!' he commanded, before striding back to the village.

***

Sina and Moana were designed to have very similar facial features to tie them together as mother and daughter. JIN KIM / DIGITAL

Moana was alone when her mother found her on the beach. Moana told her mother that she didn't suggest going beyond the reef because she wanted to be on the ocean.

'But you still do,' Sina replied.

Sina told Moana that her father was hard on her because he used to be like her. His longing for the ocean lead him beyond the reef. A friend had begged Tui to allow him to sail with him, and while they were battling against a storm, his friend fell into the water. Tui could not save him. Sina said her father was hoping to save her from this experience.

'Sometimes who we wish we were, what we wish we could do, it's just not meant to be.' Sina said.

Moana wished she could be the daughter her parents wanted her to be.

Moana longs to explore the ocean but feels the responsibility of her duties on the island.
JIN KIM / GRAPHITE, DIGITAL PAINTOVER

Modern Classics

On her way back to the village, Moana saw people happy with their lives on the island and hoped she could be happy, too. Moana climbed the sacred mountain and picked a stone to place on top of her father's, but instead of laying it down, Moana looked towards the ocean. Moana felt she couldn't deny the voice inside her a moment longer.

Moana ran to the shore. There, she found Pua sitting on a boat, holding an oar in his mouth. Moana climbed aboard.

Determined to find more fish, Moana sailed towards the menacing wave that marked the reef. Suddenly, wind filled the sail, taking the boat over the wave and past the reef. But the wave knocked Pua overboard. Moana paddled to rescue him as a mightier wave tossed her into the sea.

Moana swam to Pua and placed him onto some floating wreckage, but the waves kept coming. A wave threw Moana onto the reef, where coral trapped her leg.

Struggling below the surface, Moana grabbed a rock and smashed herself loose. She made it to shore, but the boat was destroyed and Pua was frightened.

'Whatever just happened... blame it on the pig!' Gramma Tala said, smiling.

Pua is a Kunekune pig, a small breed from New Zealand with long hair and a round build. **Bill Schwab / Digital**

[Illustration]

The wide and varied culture of the Pacific Islands is woven into every part of the story of *Moana*.
ANNETTE MARNAT / DIGITAL

Moana was worried her grandmother would tell her father what she had done, but Gramma Tala said she would not.

Moana said her father was right, and that what happened was a sign that it was time for her to place her stone on the mountain.

Gramma Tala told Moana to do it now. Then Gramma Tala walked into the ocean to dance with the manta rays.

Moana asked why Gramma Tala didn't try to stop her.

'You said that's what you wanted,' Gramma Tala replied. But as Moana turned to go, Gramma Tala told her that when she died she wanted to come back as a manta ray. Moana thought Gramma Tala was acting strangely and asked if she wanted to tell her something.

'Is there something you want to hear?' Gramma Tala replied.

Gramma Tala told Moana that she had one more story to share with her. She led Moana into the forest, to the entrance of a cave. Gramma Tala told Moana she would find the answer to who she was meant to be inside.

'Go inside... bang the drum...' Gramma Tala said.

Inside the cave Moana found a lagoon filled with ships many times the size of the fishing boats on the island. Amazed at the sight, Moana climbed aboard the largest ship to explore. There she found a drum.

When Moana struck the drum a boom echoed around the cave. Moana struck the drum again. Then Moana pounded a rhythm. The beat thrummed around the cave, waking the magic within. Torches aboard the ships blazed into life revealing stories painted on their sails. The stories were about a voyaging people who harnessed the wind to explore the ocean in search of islands. To navigate, these voyagers mapped the stars.

The voyagers took their maps with them and passed them from one generation to the next. The voyagers were Moana's ancestors.

'We were voyagers!' Moana cried, running from the cave.

The Cavern of the Wayfinders is hidden inside a lava tube. The canoes have been stored here, unmoved, for hundreds of years. IAN GOODING / DIGITAL

Modern Classics

Gramma Tala told Moana that when Maui stole the heart, a darkness fell across the world. Te Kā awoke and the ocean filled with monsters. To protect their people, ancient chiefs forbade them from setting sail and hid their ships.

Over time, people forgot that they were voyagers, but that didn't stop the darkness from spreading. It was this darkness that was sucking the life out of the island.

Moana and her grandmother have a very strong relationship. She encourages Moana to follow her heart and journey to save Te Fiti. **Jin Kim / Digital**

Gramma Tala said one day someone would sail across the ocean, find Maui and restore the heart.

Gramma Tala gave Moana a shining green stone – the heart of Te Fiti – the very same stone the ocean had given her long ago. Gramma Tala said she saw the ocean choose Moana.

As Gramma Tala spoke a wave rose up to look at them. Moana had thought it was a dream. The wave dumped water onto Moana's head and she laughed.

Gramma Tala pointed to a constellation in the shape of a fishhook and said that if Moana followed the stars, she would find Maui.

Moana didn't understand why she was chosen when she couldn't get past the reef, but then she remembered someone who had.

***

In the village, people gathered to tell Chief Tui that they were worried about the destruction they saw on the island. Chief Tui asked for calm, but before he could say more, Moana burst into the fale.

'We can stop the darkness!' Moana cried. 'And save our island!'

MODERN CLASSICS

Moana shared her grandmother's story and what she had seen in the cave. She told them that they could take the boats to find Maui and make him restore the heart.

Chief Tui glared at Moana before storming out of the meeting. Moana followed him to explain, but her father didn't want to listen.

Chief Tui picked up a torch and told her that he should have burned the boats a long time ago. Moana showed him the heart her grandmother had given her, but her father told her that it was just a rock and threw it into the forest.

Moana went to search for the heart and found it next to Gramma Tala's walking stick.

Suddenly, a horn sounded and a man ran towards them.

The necklace Chief Tui wears is made from whale teeth which only royalty would wear.
BILL SCHWAB / DIGITAL

Disney Moana

'Chief! It's your mother,' he said.

Moana and her father raced back to Gramma Tala's fale. Gramma Tala was very sick.

Moana knelt at her grandmother's side. Gramma Tala told Moana she must leave. Moana wanted to stay, but Gramma Tala said the ocean had chosen her to find Maui.

Gramma Tala gave Moana a locket to keep the heart safe. She told Moana that her spirit would follow her wherever she went. 'Go!' Gramma Tala said.

Moana fastened the locket around her neck and ran.

Moana hurried to collect supplies. As she packed, Sina appeared at her door but instead of stopping her, her mother helped her gather what she needed.

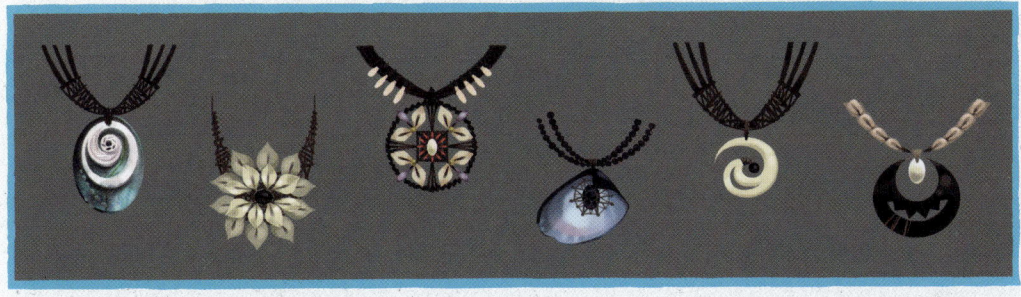

Moana's locket was given to her by Gramma Tala and holds the heart of Te Fiti. This image shows several possible designs. **Brittney Lee / Digital**

MODERN CLASSICS

Moana stowed her supplies in the canoe before pushing it into the water and sailing towards the open ocean. As Moana looked back at the village, the fires and torches went out as a wind whooshed to the shore. When it reached the ocean, the wind transformed into a glittering manta ray and swam beneath her boat. The spirit of Gramma Tala was showing her the way.

The manta led Moana to the wave that marked the edge of the reef. With her grandmother's help, Moana cleared the wave and found calm water beyond. Following the fishhook shaped constellation above, Moana sailed into the night.

Heihei is a bantam rooster based on a specific breed found on the Pacific Islands.
BILL SCHWAB / DIGITAL

The next morning, Moana heard thudding coming from inside her boat. She shrieked when a coconut emerged from the hold. Moana removed the coconut to reveal her friend Heihei.

Heihei looked and saw that he was surrounded by ocean. The confused

Heihei's character was designed to be sharp, pointy and angular to contrast with Pua's cuddliness.
ADAM GREEN / ANIMATION POSE

rooster squawked loudly. Moana replaced the coconut and Heihei went quiet but when Moana removed the coconut, Heihei screamed again. When Moana told Heihei the ocean was her friend, Heihei marched overboard. Moana dived in to rescue him and when she emerged, her boat was drifting away.

When back on board, Moana put Heihei back in the hold to keep him safe.

Moana sailed throughout the day, but as night fell, she drifted off to sleep. A wave tapped Moana on the shoulder. When she awoke, she could not see the fishhook in the sky. She'd drifted off course. Moana tried to steer, but the boat capsized and she fell into the water. Desperate, Moana begged the ocean for help.

Visual development artist Lisa Keene developed a visual language to represent the ocean's different emotional states, including anger, as shown above.
LISA KEENE / DIGITAL

Suddenly, a bolt of lightning streaked across the sky. The wind grew stronger and waves tossed Moana and her canoe.

'Help me!' Moana cried, and she looked up to see a towering wave about to crash over her.

***

Moana woke, covered in sand, on what looked like a deserted island. Moana was relieved to find her locket was still there.

Sure that the heart was safe, Moana marched into the ocean to shout at it. Moana was angry that instead of helping her, the ocean had beached her boat.

Further up the beach, Heihei walked into a boulder. When Moana examined the boulder, she saw it was covered in hundreds of scratches – tally marks arranged in the shape of fishhooks.

'Maui?' Moana asked the ocean.

The ocean raised itself into a wave and pointed. Moana turned as a hulking shadow moved across the rock. It was Maui.

Moana hid behind her boat and practised her speech.

'I am Moana of Motunui...' she said. 'You will board my...'

'Boat! A boat!' Maui cried, lifting the boat. Maui shrieked when he saw Moana below the boat. The boat dropped to the sand.

Maui is a demigod who is famous throughout the Pacific Islands. He is known as a strongman, a trickster, a shapeshifter and a champion of man. **Ryan Lang / Digital**

Moana seized her moment. 'Maui, shapeshifter... demigod of the wind and sea – I am Moana of...'

But Maui stopped her. 'It's actually Maui, shapeshifter, demigod of the wind and sea... hero of men.' Maui asked her to start again.

Moana began again, only to be stopped by another correction. Moana was frustrated that Maui wasn't taking her seriously.

Maui thought Moana wanted his autograph because he was a hero. Maui seized Heihei and signed Moana's oar with his beak.

Moana grabbed Maui's ear and told him she had come to take him to restore the heart of Te Fiti. Moana tried to drag Maui to her boat, but Maui didn't budge.

Modern Classics

Maui was confused. Moana was behaving as though she didn't like him. Maui thought this was impossible. He was stuck on the island because he had been trying to help mortals, taking the heart as a gift for them. Maui thought Moana must be trying to thank him.

'Thank you?' Moana said in disgust.

'You're welcome,' Maui replied.

Early in Maui's development the character had no hair, but local consultants from Mo'orea advised they imagined Maui with a full head of hair.
Nick Orsi / Digital

Maui showed Moana his tattoos. One tattoo showed Mini Maui holding up the sky while in another Mini Maui gave mankind the gift of fire. There was a tattoo of Mini Maui pulling the sun across the sky and of Mini Maui commanding the wind to help people sail. In Maui's tattoos, crowds of people lifted their arms in thanks.

Maui said he knew Moana was thankful and that now, he was going to take her boat and sail away. Maui lead Moana to a

Local people all said Maui needed to be huge, so the team had to design a large, powerful, but believable, character. **Jin Kim / Digital**

cave and trapped her inside with boulder.

Maui was pleased, but a Mini Maui on his arm told him to go back and do what Moana said. Maui refused. He wanted to find his fishhook. Maui picked up Heihei as a snack for later and headed to the boat.

***

Inside the cave, Moana tried to move the boulder but it was too big. Moana looked for another way out and saw a statue Maui had made of himself, not far from a hole in the roof. Moana climbed the statue and pushed it over. As it fell, Moana leapt into the hole in the roof. Moana emerged from the cave in search of Maui and saw him sailing away. She leapt towards the boat, shouting.

Maui's tattoos come to life throughout the film and led the development team to a new character called Mini Maui.
BILL SCHWAB / DIGITAL

Modern Classics

Maui looked up to see Moana plunge into the ocean.

'I could watch that all day,' Maui laughed, sailing away.

The ocean pushed Moana through the water like a torpedo and placed her on the boat.

Fists clenched, Moana told Maui that this was her canoe but Maui threw her overboard. The ocean put Moana back on board. Maui jerked the boat and smiled as Moana toppled into the water. Again, the ocean put her back.

Moana told Maui that he must sail with her and restore the heart to Te Fiti. Moana showed him the heart and Maui threw it into the water.

The Kakamora were inspired by myths the team heard around Oceania.
Bill Schwab / Digital

The Kakamora wear coconuts as armour. They are the smallest characters in the film but are fierce warriors.
Bill Schwab / Digital

The ocean pitched the heart back at Maui's head. Maui leapt into the water, but the ocean picked him up and put him back on the boat.

Moana asked if Maui was afraid. Maui laughed, but Mini Maui chewed his nails. Maui said after he took the heart he was blasted from the sky and lost his fishhook. Maui took the heart because he hoped it would give people the power to create life, but instead it was a magnet for bad luck. If Moana didn't put the heart away, bad things would happen.

'You mean this heart right here?' Moana teased, jumping up and down and waving it in the air.

Suddenly, an arrow embedded itself in the canoe. Maui said it belonged to pirates called the Kakamora.

Moana turned to see a small wooden boat emerge from the mist. The boat was filled with small coconut-like creatures.

Moana thought they looked cute until the Kakamora armed themselves for battle.

The Kakamora's weapons are fashioned out of items found in their voyages across the ocean. LEIGHTON HICKMAN / DIGITAL

The small boat revealed itself to be part of an enormous ship filled with armed warriors.

Moana begged the ocean to help. Maui said they had to help themselves.

'Tighten the halyard,' Maui commanded. 'Bind the stays!'

An initial concept for the Kakamora was that they lived on an island that was weighed down on one side by all the items they had collected. **Mehrdad Isvandi / Clay scuplt, digital paintover**

But Moana didn't understand a word, she only knew what she had taught herself.

Moana begged Maui to use his powers, but Maui said that without his fishhook, he had no powers.

Arrows, fastened with ropes, thudded into the canoe as the Kakamora's ship split into three to surround them. The Kakamora climbed onto the ropes.

Moana and Maui tried to pull out all of the arrows before the Kakamora could climb aboard but there was a rope they had missed. A Kakamora dropped onto Moana's head. More followed and one grabbed for Moana's locket. The heart fell to the deck where Heihei swallowed it.

The Kakamora seized Heihei, and raced back to their ship.

'They took the heart!' Moana cried.

Maui sprang into action. Moana thought Maui was sailing after the heart, but instead he was trying to escape. Maui refused to go back, so Moana grabbed her oar and leapt onto the Kakamora's ship.

Moana swept coconut warriors aside with her oar and dodged a shower of poison darts to rescue Heihei. Then Moana took an arrow and launched it at her canoe. With Heihei between her teeth, she slid down the rope to her canoe. Heihei coughed up the heart.

Maui aimed the boat for a gap between the Kakamora's ships and they just scraped through, leaving the ships to collide into one another and sink.

The Kakamora's ships are made from coconut shells, driftwood and any objects they have found on their journeys.
MEHRDAD ISVANDI / DIGITAL

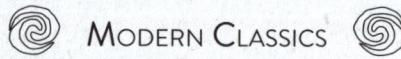

Maui congratulated Moana, but told her that he still wouldn't take the heart back to Te Fiti because of the danger they would face.

'Ever defeat a lava monster?' he asked.

'No. Have you?' Moana challenged.

Maui said the journey would mean certain death. Instead, he was going in search of his fishhook.

Moana told Maui that if he helped her, he would be a hero. Maui said he already was one, but Moana said that since he stole the heart he was the

The only way Moana can persuade Maui to help her is by journeying to find a crab named Tamatoa, and his fishhook. **Dan Cooper / Digital**

man who cursed the world. Moana said if he restored the heart, he would be everyone's hero once more.

Maui saw the crowd tattooed on his chest cheering. Maui liked the idea but told Moana the mission would be impossible without his fishhook.

Moana said they would find that first. She held out her hand to make a deal. Maui took her hand and threw her overboard. The ocean put her back.

'Worth a shot,' he said.

Maui told Moana he was sailing east to find a crab named Tamatoa, who he believed had his fishhook.

Moana asked Maui to teach her to sail there herself. Maui said he didn't think a princess was up to it.

Seeing that Moana needed help, the ocean plunged a poison dart into Maui's bottom. Maui collapsed, unable to move. Maui told Moana that she was a bad person.

'If you can talk, you can teach,' Moana replied. Moana took the oar and sailed into the night.

When Moana woke, she thought they had arrived at their destination, but when she looked, she saw Motunui.

Moana watched in horror as her mother and father ran onto the beach calling for her to help as the island, her home, collapsed into ashes before disappearing into blackness.

Moana woke from her dream to find Maui steering the canoe with the oar. Maui told her they had arrived and Moana looked up to see a towering rock.

The entrance to Lalotai, the underwater realm of monsters, is opened by a stone face. **MEHRDAD ISVANDI / CLAY SCULPT, DIGITAL PAINTOVER**

Moana asked if Tamatoa lived at the top of the rock, but Maui said it was just the entrance to Lalotai – the realm of monsters. Moana gasped in fright.

Maui told Moana to stay on the boat with Heihei because she was a chicken, just like him.

Once Maui had climbed a short way up the rock, he looked down at the boat but he couldn't see Moana. This was because Moana had climbed up ahead of him. Maui rolled his eyes and climbed after her.

Maui asked Moana why her people had chosen her for this mission. Moana explained that the ocean had chosen her and it had chosen her for a reason. Maui thought the ocean was crazy.

At the top, Moana saw no sign of an entrance.

Maui joked that first he had to make a human sacrifice. Maui blew sand off the top of the mountain to reveal a stone face. Next, Maui leapt into the air, and pounded the face with his fists.

The mouth opened and Maui leapt inside.

Moana waited until she heard a splash before she followed him into the hole. The mouth closed behind her.

Moana and Maui jump into Lalotai from the Impossible Cliff. **David Womersley / Digital**

When Maui landed in a brightly coloured cavern, he was sure there was no way Moana would follow him. Mini Maui pointed as Moana tumbled into sight. Moana crashed into Maui before bouncing deeper into the cave.

Thinking Moana hadn't survived, Maui set off to find his fishhook.

MODERN CLASSICS

The colours in Lalotai are inspired by coral, so they change as they pass through different sections of the underworld. FAWN VEERASUNTHORN / DIGITAL

But Moana had survived and was hanging, upside down, from the tongue of a fish. The fish began to pull Moana into its mouth but, before it could, the fish was gobbled up by a reef-dwelling invertebrate.

Moana unwrapped herself from the severed tongue, only to be chased by bats. When the bats passed, Moana looked around and shrieked when a glowing face appeared. The face moved closer until it was blasted into the water above by a vent.

Moana turned the corner to see a glowing entrance to a cave. As she went inside, she saw the glow was coming from a pile of treasure that was topped with a familiar-looking object.

'Maui's fishhook!' she gasped.

Moana was startled as Maui appeared behind her.

Maui told Moana to stay where she was while he went to get his fishhook. When Moana objected, Maui said that Moana had no business being inside a monster's cave. But then Maui realised he could use Moana as bait.

Dressed in glittering seashells, Moana entered the cave, banging on a drum. Moana thought the plan was silly, but Maui told her to distract the monster by getting him to talk about himself because he loved to brag.

Suddenly, Moana was lifted into the air by a giant claw and brought face to face with a jewelled crab.

The monsters found in Lalotai were inspired by real fish found in the deep sea, as well as creatures like an eight-eyed bat from the Maui legends. JIN KIM / DIGITAL

Modern Classics

'What have we here?' the crab asked, admiring Moana's costume. But when Moana's disguise fell away, the crab was disappointed to discover she was just a human.

Meanwhile, Maui crept towards his fishhook.

Suspicious, Tamatoa asked Moana why she was there.

Tamatoa is a coconut crab – they are huge, and are strong enough to crack coconuts.
BILL SCHWAB / DIGITAL

'Because you are amazing!' Moana said. Moana told Tamatoa that she wanted to know all about him.

'Are you just trying to get me to talk about myself?' Tamatoa said. 'Because if you are, I will gladly do so!'

The crab told Moana he hadn't always been shiny. He used to be dull and small. Tamatoa said Moana had probably been told to follow her heart, but this was a lie. He said searching for riches made him happy. Tamatoa said being shiny attracted fish which meant he could eat as much as he liked. Now he wanted to eat Moana.

'Hey Crabcake,' Maui shouted, swinging his fishhook. Maui tried to change into a hawk, but instead he transformed into a fish, a shark, a pig and then back into himself.

Seeing Maui's fishhook was broken, Tamatoa grabbed him and tossed him about the cave. Tamatoa picked up Moana and put her in a cage on the cave floor.

Tamatoa taunted Maui, telling him he only wanted to be a hero because he was abandoned by his mortal parents as a child. Tamatoa said Maui wanted mortals to love him because his parents never had.

Meanwhile, Moana climbed out of the cage and landed in glowing green algae. This gave her an idea.

Tamatoa was about to eat Maui when Moana held out a shining green rock.

'The heart of Te Fiti.' Tamatoa gasped, dropping Maui.

Moana ran but dropped the rock into a crack in the floor.

While Tamatoa dug for the heart, Moana snatched the fishhook and ran to Maui.

'What about the heart?' Maui said. Moana showed him the heart was still in the locket.

When Tamatoa found the rock, it was nothing more than a barnacle.

'Come back here!' Tamatoa cried.

Moana and Maui ran. They climbed to the top of a vent which fired them to safety. Maui shapeshifted as he flew.

When they landed, Maui wanted to tell Moana how much she impressed him, but Moana was distracted. Maui wondered why she was looking at him so strangely when he noticed that he was half demigod, half shark.

DISNEY MOANA

Maui said that even though Moana had helped him, he couldn't return the favour without the power of his fishhook.

An early interpretation of Maui's transformation into half demigod, half shark. DALE BAER / DIGITAL

As Moana sailed, she asked Maui if he would try. Maui moved his arm to touch his fishhook and said, 'Giant Hawk.' Once again, he shifted between an array of ridiculous creatures. Maui groaned.

Moana asked Maui about a tattoo on his back of a woman throwing a baby into the sea.

With his fishhook in hand, Maui is able to transform into different animals at will. GUILLAUME FESQUET / DIGITAL

Maui said it was none of her business. Moana asked if it was why Maui's fishhook wasn't working. Maui threw Moana into the sea.

The ocean returned Moana to the boat. Moana said she had what she needed to save her island. She told Maui she wanted to help him, too, but he had to tell her what was wrong. Maui told Moana that his human parents cast him into the sea when he was born. Maui said the gods rescued him and gave him his fishhook, making him Maui, the demigod. When Maui returned to the human world he did everything he could to make people love him, giving them land, fire and coconuts, but nothing he did was enough.

Moana said she thought the ocean chose Maui and took him to the gods because he was special.

Maui's fishhook is decorated with scrimshaw, carvings and engravings on bone or ivory, that reflect his personality. **Manu Arenas / Digital**

Moana told him that the gods didn't make him Maui, he did.

Mini Maui gave Maui a hug. Maui patted Mini Maui and told him he loved him.

Maui tried his fishhook again.

Maui's blocky head shape and expressive eyebrows bring his personality to each creature.
SERGI CABALLER GARCIA / DIGITAL

He started small, turning into a bug. It worked! Heihei gobbled him up.

Then Maui turned himself into a lizard and pitched Heihei into the sea. The ocean returned Heihei. Maui dived into the water and emerged as a shark before becoming a giant hawk. Maui swooped around the canoe, darting between rocks before cutting off their tops with his fishhook. Then Maui transformed into a whale and splashed down, drenching Moana with water. Back on the boat, Maui gave Moana a high five.

'Next stop, Te Fiti,' Moana said. She gave Maui the oar, but he gave it back – he would teach Moana how to sail there herself.

As they sailed, Maui taught Moana everything from tying knots to navigating by the stars. Moana listened closely, soaking up all of the information.

As they were sailing through fog, Maui told Moana that he knew why the ocean had chosen her.

Maui said that the ocean had liked it when he pulled up islands because people would sail through her water to find them. Maui said that if he was the ocean he would choose someone like Moana to start that again.

Moana said that this was the kindest thing Maui had said since they met but wondered why he didn't save it until they arrived at their destination.

'I did,' Maui replied, as an island belching flames and smoke emerged from the fog; Te Fiti.

Moana took the heart and gave it to Maui.

'Go save the world,' Moana told him.

Maui transformed into a hawk and set off towards the island.

As Maui flew, fireballs zoomed at him and he darted between them. Suddenly, the enormous fire monster, Te Kā, emerged from the smoke, and knocked the fishhook from Maui's hand.

Maui caught his fishhook as he fell and returned to hawk form, only to be swatted again by the monster. This time, Maui dropped the heart. Maui quickly transformed into a shark and gobbled it up.

Maui changed into a small fish to make himself harder to catch as he swam back to the boat. Moana watched Te Kā put her hand into the ocean, and saw her recoil.

DISNEY MOANA

When Maui was back on board, Moana sailed towards Te Kā. Maui told her to stop, but she thought she could make it. Maui fought Moana, but she would not give in. Maui turned as Te Kā lifted her fist to strike the boat.

The visual development, effects and animation teams worked closely together to turn a volcano into a believable and imposing character. **Ian Gooding / Digital**

Maui stopped Te Kā, but the force of the fishhook colliding with the monster blasted the canoe far from the island.

When Moana came around, Maui had his back to her. Moana asked Maui if he was okay, but when Maui turned around she saw that his fishhook was broken. Maui was angry that Moana hadn't turned back.

Moana said they could fix the fishhook, but Maui said that was impossible because it was made by the gods.

Moana said that they would be more careful next time. The monster couldn't go in the water so they needed to find a way around. But Maui said he wasn't going back. He didn't want to risk his fishhook because he believed he was nothing without it.

Moana said this wasn't true. Maui had to go back – they were only in this situation because he stole the heart.

Maui countered that they were there because the ocean told Moana she was special and she believed it. Maui wasn't prepared to die because Moana had something to prove.

Moana said the ocean had chosen her and held out the heart, but Maui said it chose wrong.

Maui used the fishhook to transform into a hawk and flew away.

'Why did you bring me here?' Moana asked the ocean. Moana begged the ocean to choose someone else. She held out the heart and the ocean took it back.

 DISNEY MOANA

Alone and far from home, Moana wept. Suddenly a light appeared in the ocean. A glowing manta ray circled the boat.

'You're a long way past the reef,' Gramma Tala said, appearing on the boat.

The two women embraced. Moana told her grandmother that she had done everything she could, but the task was too hard. Gramma Tala said she should never had asked her to do so much. If Moana wanted to go home, she would go with her.

These colour keys show Moana after defeat by Te Kā. When Maui leaves, Moana feels more alone than ever. **Andy Harkness / Digital**

But something was stopping Moana from sailing away.

'Why do you hesitate?' Gramma Tala asked.

Moana didn't know. Gramma Tala told Moana it was the voice inside her and asked Moana if she knew who she was.

Moana thought hard and listed what she knew. She was a chief's daughter from an island far away. She was someone who loved her people and the ocean. Someone the ocean called to. She was a descendent of ancient travellers. Ancient travellers that called to her, too.

As Moana thought, the apparition of an ancient ship appeared, sailing beside her. Onboard this ship her ancestor, the chief from her vision in the cave, gave Moana a gesture of respect.

As Moana began to understand who she was, she realised that the call of the ocean and her ancestors was a call she could not escape because it was inside of her. It was who she was. As Moana listened to the call, her canoe was joined by a fleet of ships belonging to her ancestors.

Moana thanked Gramma Tala for reminding her of her purpose.

Moana dived into the ocean, pushing deep below the surface. She picked the glowing heart off the sea floor. When Moana surfaced, the ships and Gramma Tala were gone.

 Disney Moana

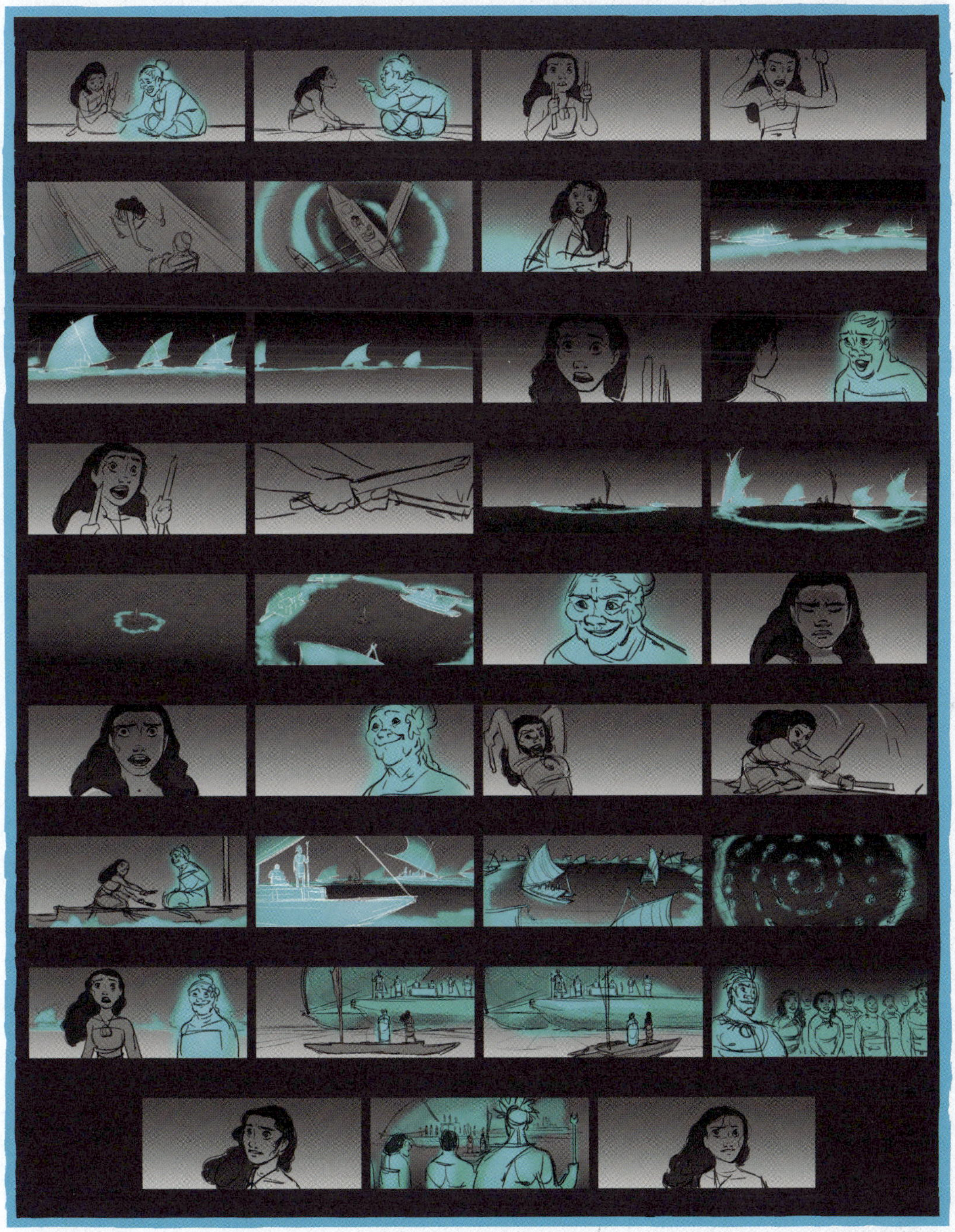

The appearance of Gramma Tala and her ancestors reminds Moana of her purpose to restore Te Fiti and help her people. DAVID DERRICK / DIGITAL

Te Kā has a recognisable female face but by playing with proportions and features, she takes on a supernatural quality. **Kevin Nelson / Digital**

Moana got to work, mending her canoe and preparing to set out alone.

Moana used what Maui had taught her to sail back to Te Fiti. Ash rained from the sky as the black island appeared on the horizon.

Moana told Heihei that this time she planned to sail around the barrier islands to reach Te Fiti and escape Te Kā.

As Moana drew closer, Te Kā emerged. Moana sailed out of reach of Te Kā, swerving to avoid the fireballs. Moana manoeuvred the boat with skill. The monster waited for Moana to approach, avoiding the water, but when she thought Moana was close by, Te Kā could not find her. Te Kā looked around to see that Moana was sailing in the opposite direction.

As Moana steered the boat between the barrier islands, Te Kā fired at the islands, hoping to sink Moana's canoe. Rocks fell all around Moana, knocking her down. As Moana fell, the heart came loose and bounced across the deck. Heihei clucked after it. Moana thought that Heihei would swallow it, but instead he gave it to Moana.

Moana wasn't out of danger. Te Kā's anger caused a wave that capsized the canoe. Moana swam back to her boat and the monster reached a fiery hand towards her. Suddenly Maui appeared as a hawk and severed the monster's arm with his fishhook.

Moana was happy to see her friend, but worried the monster would destroy his fishhook.

'Te Kā's got to catch me first,' Maui said, smiling.

Maui eventually returns to help Moana defeat Te Kā. **Kevin Nelson / Digital**

Maui said it was time for Moana to go save the world.

'Thank you,' Moana said.

'You're welcome,' Maui replied.

Maui transformed into a bug to fly at Te Kā before turning into a whale, plunging into the ocean and dousing it in water. Te Kā swatted at him but Maui escaped, turning into a hawk and severing Te Kā's arm. Maui leapt to the other arm and cut it off too, before Te Kā batted Maui onto a rock and spotted Moana sailing away.

Maui cried out to Moana as a fireball sailed towards her canoe. This time the ocean sent a wave as it capsized the ship. The ocean carried Moana on to the shore of Te Fiti.

'Get the heart to the spiral!' Maui called.

Maui turned to face the monster, leaping at Te Kā. As they met there was a mighty explosion – Maui was thrown to Te Fiti, his fishhook nothing more than a stump.

Moana looked on but couldn't stop climbing. When she reached the top of the island, she looked to where she thought Te Fiti would be, but there was no sign of the island. Te Fiti was gone.

Moana looked back at Te Kā and noticed a spiral on the fiery monster's chest. Moana gasped.

'Te Kā!' Maui cried, ready to fight. Te Kā raised a fireball to throw at Maui but stopped when a green light lit up the sky. Te Kā looked over to see the light shining from something in Moana's hand.

Early development work of Te Kā used dripping lava as hair but the team felt it was distracting. **Ryan Lang / Digital**

Modern Classics

After Moana restores the heart, it is revealed that Te Kā is in fact Te Fiti and life is restored to the island. RYAN LANG / DIGITAL

Moana told the ocean to let Te Kā come to her. The ocean obeyed, parting its waters to make a path. Te Kā screamed and rushed towards Moana, but Moana showed no fear. She walked towards the monster as the ocean rose around her, just as it had all those years ago.

Moana told Te Kā that she had travelled a long way to find her. Moana knew Te Kā wasn't a monster. She touched her hand to Te Kā's face and told her she knew who she was.

Moana placed the heart into the fiery spiral on Te Kā's chest. The spiral slowly turned green as plants sprang from its centre. Te Kā's rocky surface crumbled to reveal lush foliage – a beautiful island goddess.

'Te Fiti,' Moana said, and the goddess smiled. Te Fiti walked towards the ash-covered island and lay down, transforming it into a paradise.

A wave picked up Moana and took her to Maui on Te Fiti.

Moana told Maui she was sorry about his fishhook.

Suddenly, the earth moved beneath them. Te Fiti lifted them up to look at them more closely. Maui laughed nervously. Te Fiti glared at Maui – the demigod who stole her heart. Maui told the goddess he was sorry for what he had done.

Te Fiti smiled at Maui and held out a brand new fishhook.

Maui hesitated, but Moana said it would be rude to refuse a gift from a goddess.

The lush vegetation on Te Fiti was based on real plants, flora and fauna found in Oceania.
SCOTT WATANABE / DIGITAL

'CheeHoo!' Maui cried, before thanking Te Fiti.

Te Fiti had something for Moana, too. On the beach, the goddess conjured a blizzard of flowers and inside the blizzard was Moana's boat.

Her work done, Te Fiti lay down and became the beautiful island she had been before.

Maui helped Moana gather supplies for her voyage home and she told Maui that her people could use a talented wayfinder like him.

Maui said that they already had one and pointed to a new tattoo on his chest of a woman sailing across the ocean. Moana hugged Maui as they said goodbye.

'See you out there, Moana,' Maui said, transforming into a hawk and flying away.

Moana set sail for Motunui.

On Motunui, Chief Tui noticed something was happening. The island was coming back to life. Chief Tui looked to the ocean and saw Moana's boat appear over the reef line. Delighted, he ran to the beach to meet her.

The boats in *Moana* are based on double-hulled canoes used by the ancient Polynesians to make long journeys. **James Finch / Digital**

 Disney Moana

'I may have gone a little way past the reef,' Moana said as she embraced her parents.

'It suits you,' her father replied. The villagers, and Pua, rushed to greet her.

Before Moana returned to the village the ocean parted its waves to give her a shell. Moana took the shell up to the mountain and put it on top of her father's stone.

With her grandmother in her heart, and Maui near at hand, Chief Moana taught her people all that she had learned. The people of Motunui became ocean voyagers once more, discovering new islands and finding new homes.

The Art of Disney Moana

Moana is Walt Disney Animation's 56th feature film, directed by Disney veterans Ron Clements and John Musker. There are thousands of islands and island nations in the Pacific Ocean and Pacific Islanders often refer to them as one area, Oceania. A team travelled to the area, visiting different islands and met with researchers, teachers, experts in traditional dance and music, fishermen, navigators, elders and families to get a true sense of the culture and traditions. *Moana* was one of the most technically challenging films the Walt Disney Animation Studios had ever created and the team had to create new tools specifically for the film, including how to recreate Pacific Islanders thick, wavy hair, and Maui's many transformations. *Moana* was released in 2016 to critical acclaim and was a box office sensation. The film received two Oscar® nominations for Best Animated Feature and Best Original Song.

It is common for women and men from the Pacific Islands to wear their hair in a topknot.
BILL SCHWAB / DIGITAL

Disney Studio Artists

NEYSA BOVÉ

Concept art on pages 2-3, 67 and 70-71.

ANDY HARKNESS

Concept art on pages 4 and 9. Clay sculpt on page 9. Colour key on page 53.

JIN KIM

Concept art on pages 8, 18, 19, 24, 32, and 43.

BILL SCHWAB

Concept art on pages 10, 20, 26, 28, 33, 34, 44, 64 and 66.

BRITTNEY LEE

Concept art on page 27.

CHRIS WILLIAMS

Storyboard on pages 12-13.

KEVIN NELSON

Concept art on pages 14-15, 56 and 57.

BOBBY PONTILLAS

Concept art on page 16.

NICK ORSI

Concept art on pages 16, 17 and 32.

ANNETTE MARNAT

Concept art on pages 21 and 68-69.

IAN GOODING

Concept art on pages 22-23 and 50-51.

ADAM GREEN

Animation pose on page 28.

LISA KEENE

Concept art on page 29.

RYAN LANG

Concept art on pages 31, 58-59 and 60.

Modern Classics

Leighton Hickman
Concept art on page 35.

Mehrdad Isvandi
Clay sculpt, digital paintover on pages 36 and 40. Concept art on page 37.

Dan Cooper
Concept art on page 38.

David Womersley
Concept art on page 41.

Fawn Veerasunthorn
Concept art on page 42.

Guillaume Fesquet
Concept art on pages 46–47.

Dale Baer
Concept art on page 47.

Manu Arenas
Concept art on page 48.

Sergi Caballer Garcia
Concept art on page 49.

David Derrick
Storyboard on page 55.

Scott Watanabe
Concept art on page 61.

James Finch
Concept art on pages 62–63.

Ancient wayfinders would take pigs and chickens with them on voyages to new islands.
Bill Schwab / Digital

Moana's ceremonial outfit is inspired by the *taualuga* ceremony in Samoa. The bodice and skirt is made of *tapa* and covered in pandanus leaves, feathers and cowrie shells.
NEYSA BOVÉ / DIGITAL

An early drawing of sixteen-year-old Moana, before the team came up with the final design.
Annette Marnat / Digital